For Ozzy and Billy.

Happy memories of school days together.

Bloomsbury Publishing, London, Oxford, New York, New Delhi and Sydney

First published in Great Britain in 2016 by Bloomsbury Publishing Plc
50 Bedford Square, London, WC1B 3DP

Text and Illustrations copyright © Sam Lloyd 2016
The moral rights of the author/ illustrator has been asserted

A CIP catalogue record for this book is available from the British Library

ISBN 978 1 4088 6879 9 (HB)
SBN 978 1 4088 6880 5 (PB)
ISBN 978 1 4088 7200 0 (eBook)

Printed in China by Leo Paper Products, Heshan, Guangdong

1 3 5 7 9 10 8 6 4 2

www.bloomsbury.com

All papers used by Bloomsbury Publishing are natural, recyclable products
made from wood grown in well-managed forests.
The manufacturing processes conform to the
environmental regulations of the country of origin

BLOOMSBURY is a registered trademark of Bloomsbury Publishing Plc

# First Day
## at
# BUG SCHOOL

## Sam Lloyd

BLOOMSBURY
LONDON OXFORD NEW YORK NEW DELHI SYDNEY

At the bottom of the garden,
where no one really sees,
a secret school is hidden
amongst the grass and weeds.

Listen...can you hear it?
A tiny school bell rings...

"Welcome," smiles Miss Bumblebee, "to all you creepy, slimy things."

"It's your first day at Bug School,
but don't be scared or shy.
You'll have the BEST TIME EVER!
So wave mummy and daddy bye bye."

It's time to take the register.
Miss Bumblebee puts on her glasses.
Then, when that's done, the time has come,
to take everyone to their classes.

In Spider Class little Sid
learns to creep about.
But Mr Wincey warns him,
"Don't go up a water spout!"

In Music Class, Chloe Cricket
sings loudly through the day.

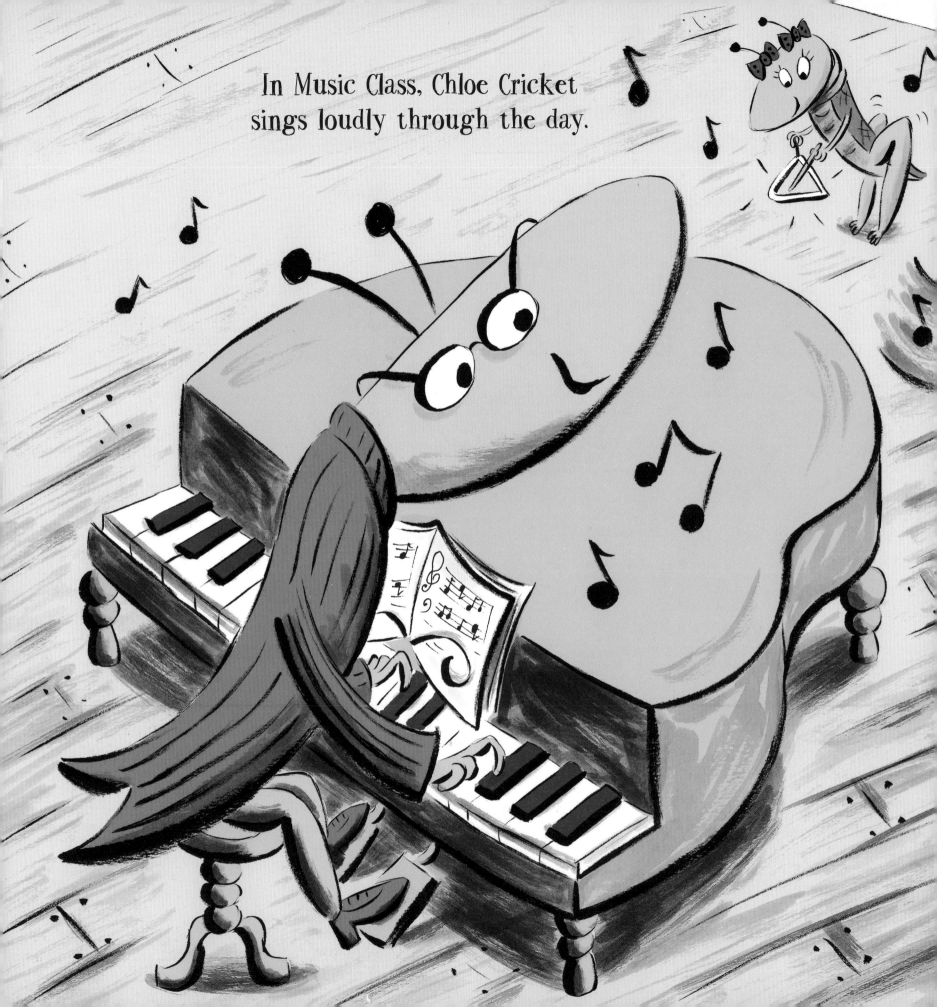

She's learning a new song
for the Bug School summer play.

Lucy Ladybird is learning maths
by counting her friend's spots.
It's so very lucky that
he's got LOTS AND LOTS!

Today's menu
Veggie option
= leaf Salad
Meat option
= aphid Stew
For Flies only
= Poop Pie

Meat

Veggie

Pud

Yummy! It's time for Bug School lunch. The ants will help you with your tray.

And, when it's all been eaten up,
you can go outside to play.

There are things to climb on,
things to slide on,
things to squash
and mend.

Golden Time
William Wasp ✗
throwing sand
Lucy Ladybird ✓
being kind

And little
Daisy Dragonfly
has made a
brand new friend.

In the toilets Sylvester Snail
is being oh so slow!
Billy Beetle bangs on the door,
"Be quick! I need to go!"

Fergus Fly mucks about,
tickling Stink Bug's belly.

"Poo! Let's get out of here —
bug toilets are SO smelly!"

Freddie Flea is so excited –
it's time to do P.E.

"Hopping, skipping, jumping.
It's the perfect class for me!"

Gosh - it's story time already,
about a super little slug.
Hurry now, Kevin Caterpillar,
and settle quietly on the rug.

Then, listen, can you hear it?
A tiny school bell rings...

...It's time to say bye-bye
to these clever little things.
All the bugs at Bug School
have had such a lot of fun.

"Can we come

again tomorrow?"

shouts out everyone.